2007

Mini Saga Competition

Young Writers

in association with

STAEDTLER

mini

S·A·G·A·S·

Fiction from Yorkshire

First published in Great Britain in 2008 by
Young Writers, Remus House, Coltsfoot Drive,
Peterborough, PE2 9JX
Tel (01733) 890066 Fax (01733) 313524
All Rights Reserved

Disclaimer
Young Writers has maintained every effort
to publish stories that will not cause offence.
Any stories, events or activities relating to individuals
should be read as fictional pieces and not construed
as real-life character portrayal.

Foreword

Young Writers was established in 1991, with the aim of encouraging the children and young adults of today to think and write creatively. Our latest secondary school competition, 'Mini S.A.G.A.S.', posed an exciting challenge for these young authors: to write, in no more than fifty words, a story encompassing a beginning, a middle and an end. We call this the mini saga.

Mini S.A.G.A.S. Fiction from Yorkshire is our latest offering from the wealth of young talent that has mastered this incredibly challenging form. With such an abundance of imagination, humour and ability evident in such a wide variety of stories, these young writers cannot fail to enthral and excite with every tale.

Contents

Zakaria Muslim Girls High School

The Mini Sagas

St George's Story

He clambered up the mountain. He was slipping and sliding but finally he reached the cave. Sword ready to slash, shield held up high, ready to slay the dragon. The cave was empty. There was nothing but a small lizard, eating a fly, in the corner.

Oliver Wilkin (12)
Corpus Christi Catholic College

11

Love Romance

The hurt inside of her, telling herself she was loved.
She was trying to cheer herself up!
He told her she was the only one for him but it was
all lies she thought. She was confused, her head was
spinning. Was their love about to end?

Laura Heaney (12)
Corpus Christi Catholic College

12

Pirates Of America

Captain Jack Pigeon walked on to the ship carefully avoiding the crew and grabbed the chest. He crept back to his crew.

'I've got it boys, from the frying Dutch man, the Davy Jones' chest meal, with fries and Coke.'

'Did I get an action figure?'

Conor Bardsley (12)
Corpus Christi Catholic College

13

The Mailbox

David and his girlfriend were having tea. There was a knock at the door. A policeman was bursting into tears,
'I'm sorry, I've just run over your mailbox.'
David was laughing, 'We don't even have a mailbox.'
A woman started to cry, 'What about my fascia objects,' said the woman.

Ben Kenworthy (13)
Corpus Christi Catholic College

14

Is Santa Here

On Christmas Eve a little girl was waiting up in her room. She heard a noise, she looked up, there was nothing there. She was wishing Santa was there. A bang came from the fireplace, the biscuits disappeared. Presents that were once under the tree were gone. A burglar left.

Jenny Nicholson (13)
Corpus Christi Catholic College

The Churchyard Grave

I was going to see my sister, Joanna. She had died five days before now. I was told she was buried near my auntie's grave.
When I arrived at the grave, Joanna was sat looking at me, but I thought she was dead.

Niamh Glynn (11)
Corpus Christi Catholic College

Untitled

One cold Christmas night, Santa and his elves were wrapping up presents when they heard a thud at the front of the sleigh. It was Rudolph, he had fallen on top of three big presents and had broken them. Santa was furious and had to give Rudolph a verbal warning.

Vanessa McDonnell (13)
Corpus Christi Catholic College

Clifford The Big Red Dog

One day Clifford, the big red dog went to the park. He started digging in the sand. The hole was getting bigger and bigger as he went further in. He came across something yellow that made a squeaking noise. When we pulled it out it was a little rubber ducky!

Bethany Welch (12)
Corpus Christi Catholic College

18

Pig Can't Ffy

Yesterday I saw something amazing. I went to school and told everyone that … pigs can fly. Everyone started laughing. No one believed me! I walked out with embarrassment.

Summer Newton (12)
Corpus Christi Catholic College

Can I Stay Here?

A young girl sat on the corner of the street, alone,
cold and wet. When a lady passed and asked,
'Are you Ok?'
The girl cried, so the woman took her indoors.
The girl was warm and clean, she asked,
'Please can I stay?'
The old lady opened a cupboard …

Becky Gallagher (12)
Corpus Christi Catholic College

Cold Night

It was a cold night, I was on my way to my sister's house and some people were looking at me. I stayed at my sister's for a bit, then I went home. I looked and the people were running away.
I got in, I had been burgled.

Christopher Moran (13)
Corpus Christi Catholic College

Untitled

It was dark in the yard. I heard a rustle.
'Hello there,' I whispered.
A voice replied, 'Go away, I'm hiding.'
'Hiding, what for?'
'Police are after me, they're here, go inside you
haven't seen anything.'
I went inside.
I woke, it was light and only a weird dream.

Shaney Parr (14)
Corpus Christi Catholic College

22

Help Me

I was sitting down, watching the television.
EastEnders was on, it's my favourite soap. I heard the
door, my mum opened the door. For a minute it was
silent. I thought it was my dad. My mum screamed
for help, I thought it was one of her tricks.
'Help me!'

Ofatomi Soremekun (13)
Corpus Christi Catholic College

23

The Garage

This is a story of a 24-year-old man.
Ste woke up one day and said to himself, ' My car
deserves a make-over.'
So he took it to his local moulding shop. He told
them his details like model, 300Z etcetera and he got
it done and said ...

Wiff Taylor (13)
Corpus Christi Catholic College

Missing

I was there, in the doctor's, a young girl came to say
'hello'.
I said, 'Hi,' a bloke came and picked her up and
walked out.
The next day she was all over the news with *'Missing'*
above her.
Then I heard a knock, the police were here.

Taylor Walker (13)
Corpus Christi Catholic College

Effie's Strange Dad

One morning Ellie was at dance, a monster walked
in and started to dance. Everyone laughed. Ellie
recognised the face of the monster, it was her dad.
She went home and asked him.
'Yes, I work as a clown and a magician.'
Ellie giggled and walked to her room …

Lois Harrison (12)
Corpus Christi Catholic College

Dinner Time

The hawk, there, staring at the mouse with his strong, focused eyes. Mouse stood as still as a half-eaten ice lolly in the freezer. Both stayed incredibly still, until Mouse ran … it was on. Hawk swooped down at Mouse.
After a few tries, Hawk finally had his dinner.

Denzel Chimanga (1U)
Corpus Christi Catholic College

The Almost Genius

I have the minds of millions to aid me. I have
fountains of knowledge at my control. I have only to
think and I will know.
I'm on Google!

Feargal O'Reilly (13)
Corpus Christi Catholic College

The Leprechaun And The Fairy

'I have no friends or family. No one likes me,' cried
the leprechaun.

'I like you.'

'Well it's Christmas tomorrow, I make a great
Christmas dinner, it will be even better sharing it
with you, will you come? Please.'

'Yes, sure.'

So the leprechaun and the fairy spent Christmas
together …

Jorgie Moran (12)
Corpus Christi Catholic College

What's Behind The Door

I walked down the hall and faced the bedroom door.
I'd always been told never to go in there, but I never
knew why.
What was so bad that I couldn't see? Then I heard a
voice whisper, it was a cold voice, crying and begging.
'Please help me! Help!'

Danielle Kilroy (14)
Corpus Christi Catholic College

Unexpected Terror

I was sat on my bed when it jumped up on my
knee. This hairy monster with huge sharp teeth.
It was edging towards me, teeth dug into my skin.
screaming my head off, in came my mum, giving me a
strange look, took the rabbit from my
knocking knees.

Alexandra Gunn (14)
Corpus Christi Catholic College

The Mysterious Dream

Suddenly I have woken. Wait, where am I? It's like a sea of darkness. No way, what's that over there? It's a monster.

No! What will I do? As I run through the forest, something has happened ... What? It really was just a dream, just a dream.

Shane Monkman (14)
Corpus Christi Catholic College

32

Penalty Shoot-Out

The whistle blew, stalemate. The match was tied. Oh no! the dreaded battle of penalties. The ball, is on the spot, intense pressure. I look up, my heart pumping and my head pounding. The goal looks tiny and the keeper looks huge. I pick my spot, shoot … Goal!

Joe Cairns (14)
Corpus Christi Catholic College

The Follower

I was walking home. A man rode by on his bike,
I started to walk quicker. Then I saw the same man
ride by on his bike. I heard the bike slam down.
Then, footsteps, following me. I started to run. He
grabbed my arm …
The director said, 'Cut!'

Lauren Howells (13)
Corpus Christi Catholic College

Untitled

He walks the streets, night after night. Searching for warmth. Nobody notices, nobody cares. He taps on our door, we give him scraps of food. More and more he gains our trust, to the point where he enters our house. He is now our new pet cat, Max.

Becky Potter (13)
Corpus Christi Catholic College

35

The Last Call

Alone. *Riinngg!*
'Hello?' Nothing.
Riinngg!
'Hello?' Nothing.
Riinngg!
'Hello? Who is it?'
I'm watching you.'
I slam the phone down instantly. Petrified. Fumbling,
I try to unlock my door, intending to race to my
neighbours. I glance backwards.
A deep voice whispers into my ear,
'Look behind you.'
Too late!

Missie McLean (13)
Corpus Christi Catholic College

Hallowe'en

Children run around endlessly after one another,
bags filled with sweets. I watched them through the
window, waiting for the bell to go.
Sure enough, I heard a ring and opened the door,
with sweets ready.
A tall figure stood there, face hidden. Neighbours
heard a scream.
My last Hallowe'en!

Ayfish Power (13)
Corpus Christi Catholic College

37

The Shot

He froze with terror, clutching his gun so tight it hurt
his hands. He'd heard a noise. Was it his imagination
or was it something else? He fired. The bang shocked
him, then there was another.
He'd been hit, right in the knee, with a paintball.

Seán Kilcoyne (14)
Corpus Christi Catholic College

Zombie Warrior

I fought my way through zombies and monsters.
Shielding myself with a dustbin lid, I shot three at
once. One of them hit me with a massive force and
knocked me down.
As I killed the last one, I heard her calling,
'Turn that game off, your dinner's ready, James!'

Abigail Warwick (13)
Corpus Christi Catholic College

Rejection

All she ever did was reject me, pushing it back into
my face. I tried again but she just wouldn't keep it.
I don't know why I didn't walk away. Then I thought
to myself, *why don't I try cleaning it?*
Then I finally got the DVD to work!

Santino Browne
Corpus Christi Catholic College

Draco And Pansy

One day a dragon met a flower. He had never seen a flower as pretty before and instantly fell in love. This flower was called Pansy. The dragon went to the flower to say hello, but sent out a snort of fire. The flower went up in flames. Barbecued Pansy!

Jennifer Hurley (13)
Corpus Christi Catholic College

41

Worst Fear

A single tear rolls down my cheek and I wipe it away
furiously. I'm not going to let him see me cry.
I thought I could trust him! It's going to hurt. Well,
I'm not going to let him do it again!
I scream out. God, I hate the dentist's.

Megan Gaughan (13)
Corpus Christi Catholic College

42

Gone

Rushing around, getting ready. Tonight's our anniversary. I can't wait. Oh, look at the time! Do I look okay? Will he like this dress? *Knock, knock.* Oh, no time for that, he's back from work.
I open the door.
The police, 'There's been an accident.'
I know instantly he's gone.

Sian Gaughan (13)
Corpus Christi Catholic College

The Attacker

I crept behind a tree in the dark, eerie forest.
Listening for my attacker, edging nearer. I longed to
run but I couldn't give myself away. I held the gun out
behind the tree. There he was, I shot …
paint hit him.
We couldn't help laughing, what fun paintballing is.

Megan Davies (13)
Corpus Christi Catholic College

The Face

I shuddered as the horrid image stared back at me,
bulging eyes, popping out of the head. Huge, pointy
nose, teeth as crooked as a burglar. Scruffy, mousy-
coloured hair, all dishevelled and out of place.
The sight was horrific!
But as the old saying goes, 'The mirror never lies'!

Bethany-Jo Ffanagan (13)
Corpus Christi Catholic College

45

The Marathon

I ran, I ran faster. I heard the people I was trying to dodge, tut and shout at me. I panted. I looked ahead, I had entered the scruffy side of town. I heard someone say, 'Rover!'
I looked behind me, the dog had stopped chasing me.

Hannah Chapman (12)
Corpus Christi Catholic College

The Race

I lost my breath as I picked up my pace. On the way
my bobble fell out. I was tempted to go back for it
but I carried on. I felt my shoelace come undone.
I was running first place, near the end.
I fell to the ground.

Becky Simmons (12)
Corpus Christi Catholic College

Escape

The gun, visible now, pumping and pounding, ranting, raving. His heart was beating at 100 beats per second. He ran through the corridor, looking back every now and again to see if his lead was still there. He came to a halt and his stomach dropped, as the shadow emerged.

Karl Hardcastle (13)
Corpus Christi Catholic College

The Long Run

Running, running, can't stop running. The thorns rubbing against his legs. Fear running through his mind. A wall of thorns in his way. Jumping into it. The points brushing on him. The unbearable pain. Turning to see the beast behind him …

Joshua Brady (12)
Corpus Christi Catholic College

Phill's Travel

Phill was walking up the street from school. He went into the corner shop and bought a Lucozade Sport for the long trip home. A bit further on he stopped again to go in the fish and chip shop. He bought a chip sandwich.
He must have walked five miles.

Liam Dolan (12)
Corpus Christi Catholic College

The Painting

I fell asleep and ended up in a white room and in that room, mounted on a wall was a canvas with a realistic painting. An abstract painting. Suddenly I woke up and Mum came in with a painting. The same abstract painting as my dream!

Donovan Doherty (12)
Corpus Christi Catholic College

Will I Ever See Them Again?

I waved to my mum and dad. I was crying out of my big blue eyes like a waterfall. I might never see them again. I was so scared, I was shaking. I went to go and ask if I would see them again and they said, 'Umm, no!'

Emily Kilby (12)
Huntington Secondary School

Heartbroken

A tear rolled down my pale yet rosy cheek. I can't believe he would do this to me. After everything we'd been through! I don't believe it! He wasn't perfect but I couldn't trust him again, not this time, anyway. I'm heartbroken, but I love him and always will.

Alex Beardsley (12)
Huntington Secondary School

Buff

'So! You've heard me, I don't want to see you again,
Max. You're just too dangerous in form. I'm afraid
I have to leave.'
'Men, fire at will now.'
'Argh! Julie help me! Don't leave me to die.'
She paused, 'Wait, don't shoot, he's innocent. Max
I love you honey.'

Ryan Mercer (12)
Huntington Secondary School

54

Dead

Looking over at him, his blue eyes shining in the sunlight. I stepped forward, crossing the road to talk to him. He had noticed me coming over. *Bang!* A bright light was shining in the distance. I wondered what it was. Then it hit me, not literally, but it did.

Katie Smith (12)
Huntington Secondary School

Humpty Dumpty Died

Humpty Dumpty ate his breakfast on that fateful day. He took off his pyjamas and got dressed. He was being teased. He sat down on a wall. He was pushed off the wall. When the army came they thought he was an egg trying to take over the world. *Bang!*

Charles Merritt (11)
Huntington Secondary School

Falling

I was falling, through the cold winter air. I was floating, down and around. I was falling towards the ground. I was twirling, round and round. The floor closed in and I felt so trapped as it came closer. I was falling down.
I had fallen all the way down.

Hannah Linaker (12)
Huntington Secondary School

57

The Day Being A Security Guard

My best friend was moving into a new house, so she had to move to a new school too. She didn't have any friends there. The reason they were all having to move was because her dad was a security guard and he was getting transferred to a different town.

Ashleigh Newsome (11)
Huntington Secondary School

In The Mist

I smelled the air … musty. Something wasn't right, the mist was so thick I couldn't see anything. I called out … nothing. I looked down at my feet, it looked like my feet didn't exist. Suddenly I heard something. Then I really wished I hadn't looked back towards that mysterious noise.

Matthew Bradbury (12)
Huntington Secondary School

Who Knows, You Decide

I've waited all my life to get to the cup final. The cup
is in sight, it is nearly ours. It's down to penalties.
I, the captain, have to score to win the match. The
referee blows his whistle, I take my shot, but the
floodlights went off …
Who's won?

Baxter Hackett (11)
Huntington Secondary School

I'm Innocent

It was stormy the day they took him away. We were everything to each other. He kept saying he was innocent. I believe he was, nobody does it on purpose. I love him, but now he's gone. 'I'm sorry for your loss Miss, but it's over for him.'

Kate Twiddle (11)
Huntington Secondary School

Bad Night's Dream

I heard a scream in my ear, when I looked around
nobody was there. The voice sounded like Katie, my
sister, but she was at her friend's house.
Probably dreaming.
'Argh, what's that? Who is it? I can't bear it anymore.'
'Emma, wake up, Emma you can wake up now.'

Effie Bellwood (11)
Huntington Secondary School

62

The Music Crisis

Mr Jennings, a music teacher, got sacked for breaking the rules. He would not let us play an instrument. Every lesson we are supposed to play. The police came to take him away. We all danced on the tables, even the teachers were happy. He is still locked away.

Abigail Stephenson (12)
Huntington Secondary School

63

The Pixie Computer Fixer

I was sitting at my computer desk, doing my Saga homework, when there was a weird noise coming from under it. I looked under and saw a little pixie. A rabbit had bitten my wires and pixie sat there fixing them.

She said, 'Finished.' And was never, ever seen again.

Aisling Cairns (12)
Huntington Secondary School

My Newt, Tiny

Yesterday I went into my garden and guess what
I found? A little newt on the ground. I called it Tiny.
I showed it to my family and friends and my dad said
to me,
'Why did you call it Tiny?'
I replied, 'Because it is my newt!' *(Minute)*.

Abigail Edgar (11)
Huntington Secondary School

The Race

I went into my starting position, I listened for the
gun, *bang!* My arms were pumping, my legs were
sprinting, my heart was beating. I heard the cheers.
I had to win, I was determined.
I crossed the line, I looked around.
'I won,' I shouted.

Kate Harris (11)
Huntington Secondary School

My Bad Nightmare

'1, 2, 3, here it comes, run before you get hurt.'
'What about you? The bad weather will blow you off
the cliff.'
Bang! Here comes thunder.
It was when I had closed my eyes, I had gone here.
I woke up in shock.

Frances Kennedy (11)
Huntington Secondary School

67

Deathbed

I was lying in a scratchy, uncomfortable bed, in a
gloomy hospital ward. I was thinking about my family.
How they had died only yesterday. I had no one.
I was worth nothing, I wanted to die. I felt I needed
to die.
Beep, beeeeeep!
I was gone! Gone forever.

Olivia Dickons (11)
Huntington Secondary School

68

Escape

I dived into the muddy water. I was swimming
slowly as I passed black shadows. No one was
there. I was alone. I was going to get away from
here to somewhere safe. I started to swim upwards,
something was grabbing my leg.
It was only seaweed!

Megan Affington (11)
Huntington Secondary School

Untitled

A beast came to the village. It made people leave.
The beast ate the village to death. The men decided
who should kill the beast. The beast attacks again,
the man lunges.
Bang! Bang! Bang! What happens no one knows!

Ben Plews (11)
Huntington Secondary School

Burning Flame

I looked out over the sea, then I saw it. It was nearing the tower. I jumped in the car and headed for the motorway. I heard screaming, I ran. There was a baby crying. I jumped in and saved it. *Boom!* the fire was rising, it caught me. Dead!

Harry Luck (12)
Huntington Secondary School

Rainbow

The sun was glaring down onto the sea. It was boiling hot. Clouds were coming across the sea. It started to rain, *plop, plop, plop*. The sun was still out. It seemed I had appeared from nowhere. Then the sun started to cool down.
I started to disappear.

Danielle Graham (11)
Huntington Secondary School

72

My Angel

Crash! Then the silence began. Pasty-white, her face turned. A shade of blue her lips went. A bright light appeared to her, peace at last.
Her name is carved on polished rock for everyone to remember and an angel looks over her grave.

Lauren Hoffy Curcher (13)
Huntington Secondary School

Kidnap

The depth of the night lay upon me like a mask of invisibility. Footsteps behind me, racing towards me. Bony hands clutched my chest tight. As a light shone on the dusky road, a deep clatter spread all around me. Then my scream faded into the depth of the night.

Rebecca Long (12)
Huntington Secondary School

The Ticking In The Night

One cold, misty night when I was sitting in my bed,
I heard a ticking noise. Suddenly I saw a man's
shadow. I looked downstairs, nothing was there.
I went downstairs and the only thing there was, was
a clock covered in blood.

Jack Heys (11)
Huntington Secondary School

The Darkness

I sat there, in the dark, holding myself. Scared to death. Shivers ran down my spine. Was it me or was it my imagination playing tricks on me again? Someone or even something was out to get me.
Is it the end?
Bang!
The light was turned on! Thank goodness.

Rubena Rahman Kamali (11)
Huntington Secondary School

The Arising Dark

The flag hung there, black and ragged. Spears and swords flung through the empty air. Loud drums boomed. Vines straggled on the floor. We had come to the rainforest. They could hide. Cries came from behind us. The darkness took me. I felt nothing, only the world fading away.

Tiffy Daish (11)
Huntington Secondary School

Train Death

I lay there, in the rain. I could hear the train coming.
It was the end of me. I tugged at the rope, this was it.
The train was getting closer. I could hear a bang, my
heart or was it?
I felt my cold chest ... nothing!

Jake Dalby (11)
Huntington Secondary School

78

It's You

That is the one. I knew it from the moment I saw her. Her eyes like melted chocolate, her tongue soft and smooth. She gazed adoringly at me and her tail wagged. We were meant for each other. I had always known it. I called her Gem. She is mine.

Rachel Burgess (12)
Huntington Secondary School

What Am I?

Lighter than a feather, only comes out when sunny.
Follows you everywhere. Dance and it will dance,
run and it will run. Do anything it will do the same. It
has no colour and is always at your feet. It's always
silent, cannot say a word.
What am I?

Emma Walton (11)
Huntington Secondary School

80

Is It Real?

That day we won.
The war had started … we marched up to the front
line. Gunshots fired. Twenty men on their side got
killed by our marine team. Fifteen of them were
alive. We went for Commander Jelly Belly.
Yes! We got him but he was too heavy to carry!

Jake Molesbury (11)
Huntington Secondary School

Me

The girl entered the church, sheltering from the rain, clutching her chest. She ran to the front and started praying. She was sad. She was mad. She killed her friend in a row. A knife could do a lot of harm. The girl was me, I stabbed myself.

Chloe Constable (11)
Huntington Secondary School

82

The Creature

I saw him there, behind the tea-chest box. I shone the light on his face. Bluebottles he ate. My heart was beating so fast, I didn't know what to do. Should I tell Dad or not? He's going to knock it down anyway. I don't know what to do!

Tiffy Carling (11)
Huntington Secondary School

Santa

'Santa, Santa, you have just got a call on the hot line,
what should we do?'
'Well answer it then you dimwit, pass it here. It's
from the President of the United States.'
'Santa, I have a big problem,
you are burning the wire out.'
Crackle, beep, beep.
'Hello!'

Alexandra Quiff (11)
Huntington Secondary School

The Multicoloured Cat

One day there was a multicoloured cat, Monty. He was the only multicoloured cat in town. None of his friends were multicoloured. He was always bullied, he was really sad. Then one day someone was painting, so Monty spilt the paint on the bullies.

Bethany Vickers (11)
Huntington Secondary School

The Title With No Name

It is dark and scary. I am petrified, really scared.
Everything is coming out at me. We are going down,
'*Argh!* I'm scared, stop! It is too scary.
Please let me out.'
We came out finally.
The ghost train was really scary after all. I wonder
what's next?

Ben Aitken (1D)
Huntington Secondary School

86

Bang! Bang!

I shouted, 'Mr Walker, no, please!'
He pointed the gun right at my head. He shot three
warning shots in the air and shouted at them to
move. He shot the ambulance man in the head. Mr
Walker gave a chuckle and pulled the trigger.
Bang! Bang! Bang!

Joshua Hebden (11)
Huntington Secondary School

Rosie The Kitten

Rosie was a troublesome kitten. One quiet evening she climbed on the worktop and stuck her furry little paws into the jam jar. She then stood up, blackflipped off the worktop and landed on Henry, the wheelchair bound chinchilla and stuck her dirty, jam stained paw in his eye.

Kathleen Knox (11)
Huntington Secondary School

Jump To The Future

It was World War Two and Private Tom jumps out of
the plane. An endless portal opens in front of him.
Next thing he knows, he is in a house. He sees a
thing called a Nintendo Wii,
'What is this thing, I think I could live with this.'

James Bareham (11)
Huntington Secondary School

89

The Wood Of Love

I entered the wood on a dark night, not knowing
where I was.
I looked round a tree and found a boy, my age. We
looked into each other's eyes, and fell into dreams.
We left the wood.
Every morning we go to the place where we met.

Kayleigh Zurek (12)
Huntington Secondary School

The Match

Newcastle United and Manchester United strode onto the horrendously boggy pitch to play the Premier League. Newcastle take the centre, the massive stadium is packed with supporters. The crowd are going wild. On the left of me supporters are making a Mexican wave.
The whistle goes to start the game.

Harry Sanderson (11)
Huntington Secondary School

Bird Poo

A boy was walking one sunny evening and looked up and saw a bird, flying high up in the sky. The bird pooed on top of his head. The boy didn't mind, he was very superstitious and believed it was good luck for a bird to poo on his head.

Megan Eastwood (12)
Huntington Secondary School

Cerry And The Crystal Glass Dragon

Cerry ran, he couldn't see what was following him. Suddenly, a burst of white, hot fire was bellowed at him. He turned around to see a dragon, made out of glass, with a flame burning inside it. Cerry conjured a magical, blue orb to protect him from the dragon's flame.

Liam Bishop (12)
Huntington Secondary School

The Waltzers

I was woken up by the spinning. I was thrown side
to side. There was screaming, shouting, machines
clanking. The barrier lifted.
A voice said, 'Please exit the Waltzer.'
I got off and then I threw up!

Adam Dunkiff (11)
Huntington Secondary School

Alive

I opened my eyes … alone, unwanted. The shadows glared at me. It's inside. A noise was coming out of the closet, I opened it. Alive, awake, I ran out the front door of the monster house. I got a lighter and threw it. *Bang!* gone, I was saved.

Jack Rowson (12)
Huntington Secondary School

Shipwreck

I go onto the ship, waiting for Mum and Dad. They
came and I hug them, then we are ready to go. Mum
and Dad got off the ship, it left the dock.
I waved to Mum.
I got stuck on an island, will I ever get off?

Karf Effis (12)
Huntington Secondary School

The Armoured Lioness

Her might was immense, blood flows more, her armour stained, her lion heart strained. Her paws swiped through the air, knocking down the men. She stands up on hind legs and roars out her heart, her teeth fierce, her claws sharp.

They were gone and she was alone once more.

Katie Cooper (12)
Huntington Secondary School

Pure Luck

I shut my eyes as the wind from the cars brushed
past my face. My little car was being pushed around.
My heart stopped as the young boy racer started
heading towards me. Then, he slowed down and
undid his seat belt.
Game over. The bumper cars have stopped.

Tomas Davis (12)
Huntington Secondary School

Oblivion

The roller coaster starts with loud, scary, terror music, before you go up and up until you're three hundred feet in the air. It turns a corner, then hangs you over the side of a drop. Then falls into oblivion. The wind gushes against your face, that's the Oblivion.

Jake Beaumont (12)
Huntington Secondary School

Worst Nightmare

I was staring into the mirror when I spotted a spider.
It was abnormal, it was somehow different. Then
more and more came out of nowhere. They were
closing in on me! I yelled for help but no one came.
They started to chant …
Suddenly I woke up!

Annie Durkin (12)
Huntington Secondary School

Living Dead

Pain, horror. My eyelids are brutally separated from my eye sockets. I will never die. My toenails have been sliced off with a knife. I feel the skin, which used to be protected by my nails, now being ripped off and run up my leg, arm and face. Blood.

Abigail Porter (12)
Huntington Secondary School

A Day As Me

I sneak up to the crowd of birds and pounce on a sparrow. Its head is crushed by my weight, so I eat it. I pick up its body and squeeze through the cat-flap. I drop it on the floor, my owner scolds me.

I'm a cat.

Jack Heels (11)
Huntington Secondary School

The Big Bang

The time was coming closer and closer, the clock was ticking … My shaking legs wobbled and my knee caps froze as I stood on my silky, pink quilt cover. Clenching my wooden bunk bed, I leapt off my bed and *bang!* I was awake.

'School!' bellowed my outraged mother!

Megan Foster (11)
Huntington Secondary School

It

I was twisting and turning, round and round, spinning like a spinning top. My tummy with butterflies inside. The world seemed to be going into the sun. Loops, twists and turns. Quickly we stopped. I was on the ride of a lifetime. The Curve. *Wow wee!*

Harry Baufch (11)
Huntington Secondary School

Forest And Back

The mighty serpent pulled its fangs from my chest.
I screamed but no one heard. The forest seemed
to laugh, as I lay dying on the dirty floor. A black
nothingness ate me whole.
Beep, beep, I sat up, my face sweating.
'Why does my chest hurt?'
Wait, what the …

Peter Savage (12)
Huntington Secondary School

Magic

I saw them in the dark. They can't fool me. Little shadow people, tiny as can be. I study them at night-time. They dance from dusk until dawn. No one else can see them except me and I'm alone.

Tirion Horn (11)
Huntington Secondary School

Dead Or Alive?

Hours after clambering down a drain, I was still
walking with no sign of a dragon. I wondered if
Grandad was psycho and a dragon living in his drain
was a fabrication. But then the tunnel ended, there
lay a dragon, my torch went out.
Was I dead or alive?

Chris Hudson (11)
Huntington Secondary School

Frozen Blood And Frozen Hearts

I remember vividly, waking up with a cold sweat,
screaming. The dream had taken me deep into the
woods at Drop Off Edge. Her face streaming with
tears - no more than twelve. She fell. Real life; I ran,
ran to Drop Off Edge, blood frozen, my heart frozen.
She awoke …

Rhiannon Nichol (12)
Huntington Secondary School

I Will Find You

You have no place to hide, you have no place to go.
I will find you!
I can see a foot-mark hidden under a layer of sand.
I will find you!
What is this? A spot of blood. I know where you are,
there is no escape now! *Ha!*

Rebecca Anderson (11)
Huntington Secondary School

My Lucky Day

There was a boy who wanted a new computer, so his mum took him to PC World. When they got there, the shop was empty. What are we going to do, they thought.

Then a lady came and said, 'Are you wanting a new computer? You can have this one.'

Nathan Bargate (12)
Huntington Secondary School

The Thing

I was walking through a dark alley, I tripped and in front of me, it scared me to death. The thing was big, scary, fluffy, ripping and scratchy. I got up and ran for my life. Then I turned and went back and saw it was a cute cat.

Stuart Garbutt (12)
Huntington Secondary School

The Shadow

I was walking home from football on Thursday, when I started to hear a rustling noise from behind me. I ignored it for a while but then it started to get on my nerves. I turned around to find a great black shadow.
'Argh!' Then I was one of them!

Grace Baron (11)
Huntington Secondary School

112

The Dog Whisperer

I am Buster, a vicious Rottweiler. I am vicious towards other dogs, so my owners decided to call Ceaser Millian the dog whisperer. When he first came I was scared as he pinned me to the floor. But now I am a sensible dog around other dogs, big and small.

Adrianne Scaife (11)
Huntington Secondary School

The Difference Between Friends

My best friend snatched my umbrella in the rain on the way home and shouted, 'Run Dork, run.' I sprinted home and stared at my hair. At that moment I realised, yeah a friend would let you borrow her umbrella but a best friend would take yours and shout run.

Elizabeth Bateson (11)
Huntington Secondary School

The Star

I glitter and glisten away in the night. I shimmer and shine and shoot across the sky. But the ebony space around me is empty and desolate, crying out for noise. Will it ever come?

Anna Chaplin (11)
Huntington Secondary School

Mealworm In Maths

Mealworm walked to school to have a maths lesson.
In it he learnt flame and gas equals explosion. So
he thought, flame and planet of gas equals huge
explosion. On his trip to Uranus he took some
matches and set Uranus alight.
(Uranus is a gas planet.)
Boom! Kaboom!

Callum Small (11)
Huntington Secondary School

Who Knows?

Who knows? Not everybody knows, unless you tell them. I know. If I know then she will know. But if she knows then he will know. But then not everybody knows. So who knows? Why did it end like this. I didn't do it.

Lily Dixon (12)
Huntington Secondary School

The Hammer

One day I was watching TV in my room and I put my feet on my drawers and they snapped. I told my dad, he flipped. He got his hammer and nails, swung down and cracked his own leg!
The doctors say it's fractured. I'm grounded. I'll get him back!

Callum Greenwood (12)
Huntington Secondary School

118

That Sinking Feeling

I'm going down into the deep water. Nobody notices, nobody cared. I'm just floating down. Nobody minds, I'm going to a better place anyway. I'm alone, floating down, down, down. I've been seen, they're bringing me up to the light. Wait a minute this isn't the river. Am I dead?

Gene Effigott-Furness (11)
Huntington Secondary School

They're Coming

The two men strode around the town, their pace getting faster. Every once in a while they would look around like they were trying to find something or someone!
The men were heading to the house! I ran downstairs just as they barged into the house! Suddenly I saw colours …

Edward Yardley (11)
Huntington Secondary School

Slime River

He was so heavy, he couldn't stand up, he couldn't breathe. He collapsed. Lying on the floor, dying. Someone was there, something was happening. But what? He knew something was there. Slime suddenly poured, like a river, out of his mouth. He passed out. The next morning he felt lighter.

Andrew Rothwell (11)
Huntington Secondary School

The Road

At the edge of the kerb I crossed the road, carelessly,
not looking, not waiting, not having a care in the
world. Suddenly a screech, blackness crept out of me
and my spirit floated away.
Up and up to the skies above.
I wish I had looked!

Sophie Maskiff (11)
Huntington Secondary School

Buffy At Three-Thirty

Oh great, three-thirty. Most people would be happy
but not me. It was time for my daily spanking. Here
he comes, closer. A shadow looms over me; big
Boris. Here comes his great, big hand, drawing
towards my bottom. Then impact!
Attacker and his victim.
The pain throbs like Hell!

Joe Phillips (11)
Huntington Secondary School

123

The Window

I gazed out of my window at the dark night sky, at
the moon that hung limply and at the silhouettes of
buildings. I saw the broad, leafless trees as they stood
proudly and the few people meandering, casting
shadows on the ground. Through the foggy glass
I saw life.

Moffy Nichols (11)
Huntington Secondary School

Mini Dog Scrap

Two dogs, old and young can't stop scrapping over the silliest things, like seaweed. On Whitby beach, two adults, two children. Doggies find a piece of seaweed, decide both want that piece, no other. As if to say give it to me, I deserve it! Then Mother steps in. Argh!

Sophie Layton (11)
Huntington Secondary School

One Eye

Borzhar roared. Foolish Khazrat had disobeyed
Heltork. No man would stop Borzhar. The horns of
his thick skull impaled a man. Bray-Shaman Darkgave
foretold this to be his day. But, what seemed to be an
impatient charge had become Khazrat's own victory.
Borzhar roared. Heltork joined the young
Foe-render …

Jack Matthews (11)
Huntington Secondary School

When Will She Come?

Days seemed endless before she came.
I stepped onto my deck, she rose to witness the
destructiveness she caused. She fell into the waters,
I peered down and noticed it was my lost mother-
in-law. I sailed off into the distant sunset, leaving her
- cold as an ice cube!

Rachel Holderness (11)
Huntington Secondary School

Decay

I could see deserted wasteland. Nothing else for miles around, other than a ruin of an industrial building and rubble, scattered around the terrain. I ran towards the building leaving the Landrover behind. A sandstorm could be whipped up by nuclear winds without warning. I needed to find a bunker.

Chris Barrett (13)
Huntington Secondary School

Girl/Boy

Arrive at school, hair straight, lipgloss on.
Arrive at school surrounded by friends and wearing a
scruffy jumper. 'Wow, who's that?' She never noticed
him before.
'Wow, she's pretty.' Her friends told her to talk to
him, his mates encouraged him. Shy glances. Swap
numbers. Together forever? Or not …

Jess Brooks (13)
Huntington Secondary School

Untitled

She was lying there, in a deathly silence, blood everywhere. No one around. Trees swaying without a sound. She cried for help but no one heard a thing. Her frozen eyes staring into the deep, black sky. She lay there dying, next to the smoking car.

Alex Kelly (12)
Huntington Secondary School

Friends Till The End

Ding dong,
'I'll get it!'
It was Kimi, my best friend. We rushed to each other and gave our usual greeting. I took her upstairs to go on our Bebo's. We laughed, we chatted and she went to the loo. I looked at her page about me. My secret.
'Kimi!'

Effie Johnson (13)
Huntington Secondary School

Seconds From Disaster

Driving down the country road, the storm raged. Forks of phantasmagoric lightning bolts reached down, striking aimlessly. The Titan's wrath struck again, illuminating a wide-eyed man - hanging from the crimson, pylon wires. Robert stared; saw the bloody face, then a car's headlights; heard his own ghastly scream - then nothing.

Craig Shutt (12)
Huntington Secondary School

I'll Miss You

Since the first day I came here I was so shy
and nervous.
Yet you came and said. 'Hi.' Today we're still friends.
Now you're leaving me, going to another country.
I hope you come back soon. Will you remember me?
I'll remember you, forever.

Imogen Galloway (13)
Huntington Secondary School

Hurricane

The wind blew hard through the city. Buildings
were being torn away. Little kids being blown down.
Screams were in the air. The hurricane was blowing
over the city, killing loads. People were running into
their homes, hiding away from it.
But, nowhere for me to go.

Alex Woodhouse (12)
Huntington Secondary School

Talkative Apple

I was sunbathing in a tree, when, I was rudely
awakened by a girl that said,
'That apple looks nice to eat.'
So I said, 'Actually I'm as sour as a lemon, so choose
another apple.'
So the little girl ran home crying, 'Mummy.'
I giggled away to myself.

Aisling Brown (11)
Huntington Secondary School

Evil

Suddenly darkness surrounds, the light is gone and
I am alone. Enchanted tendrils surround me, so when
I scream, I scream in vain. Bright sparks of evil flash,
shocking me and leaving me numb. Then, when
I thought I surely was dead; an almighty flash of light,
then darkness …

Carrie-Ann Harrison (11)
Huntington Secondary School

136

Depressed

I was depressed. Doing nothing. Thinking bad
thoughts. The dog came in, I petted him. He's
pathetic. I'm pathetic.
My friend phones, I say 'Hi.'
She goes, I fall asleep. I wake to find my sister being
shouted at.
I smile, now she's depressed.

Violet Reeves (12)
Huntington Secondary School

Spooky

The moon was thin and glowing brightly. The shadows were dark and mysterious. I walked towards the silent town and crept into a still, wooden barn. There the party began! Disco lights filled the barn. Funky music made me dance! Suddenly the lights flickered out; I was alone.

Joseph Walters (11)
Huntington Secondary School

The Darkest Night Ever

The tangy, yellow eyes watched its prey, never letting it out of sight. Its dark fur, dark as shadows, camouflaged it in the night. Then it pounced for its prey. All it saw was a horrible, sharp, external darkness.

Lewis Holmes (11)

Huntington Secondary School

The Explosion

A black blanket dominates the sky. An explosion erupts and the dark figure falls to the floor. He lay there motionless, as the flakes of burnt car brush his cheek in the moonlight. Blood gently trickles down his forehead, like water would down a valley. Then his heart stopped.

Joe Efferker (11)
Huntington Secondary School

Me, The Five Pound Note

Hi, I'm a five pound note. Most of my life I have lived in a till. It's all cramped and squished. I hate it. It didn't used to be like this. At first it was all nice and cosy in an old man's wallet but then he spent me.

Adam Copley (12)

Huntington Secondary School

141

Attack Of The Man-Eating Panda

The panda was walking down the road. It looked cute, so I walked up to it and started to stroke its soft, black and white fur. It growled at me. I thought it was hungry, I wasn't wrong. It ate me!

Conor Moore (12)
Huntington Secondary School

Shadows

It follows me everywhere, where there's light. Every movement, day or night. As I glide along the sky it changes shape and size. When I run it's there. When I swing on the swing it's there. When I turn the light off - it's gone …

Becky Aldrich (12)
Huntington Secondary School

I Change

I was rushing down the street at half a mile per hour. My heart was pounding, I'm a caterpillar. I was running from a butterfly. It was trying to eat me. Suddenly I changed into a man-eating kangaroo. I take people in my baby pouch and eat them alive.

Tom Currie (11)
Huntington Secondary School

Not Enough Petrol To Die

Plane wobbling, children shouting, bags flying from cheap overhead storage spaces. Everyone thought - doomed. Everyone felt drop, holiday over before begun. Out of the blue, plane stopped. People jumped out quick as possible, one metre to ground. Levitating like magic, it ran out of petrol.

Anastasia Pavlovets (11)
Huntington Secondary School

The Attacker

Fear was pumping through my body. Blood covering
my face. The stabbed places on my body. The
horrific growling noise. I was sure this was the end.
Why me though?
I plucked up the courage to open my eyes, to see my
five-stone bulldog licking my face.

Katie Draper (11)
Huntington Secondary School

Don't Inject Me

Standing there, alone, I was beginning to wonder if I could take the pressure. She called my name. I took a deep breath. Immense build-up, go towards the door. I was completely alone now. I sat down, she stabbed the needle in. Screams emanated from the room.

Chloe Hollows (12)
Huntington Secondary School

Mouse

I smelt the scent. I pranced, I leapt, I dodged. I let off
wind. I jumped over the sink, I climbed through the
fruit, I ran across the worktop, squeezed through
a hole in the fridge. Routed for where the piece of
cheese was.
Nibble, nibble, squeak, squeak!

Harry Osguthorpe (12)
Huntington Secondary School

Silent Street

The street went silent. All you could hear were the birds twittering at the top of the trees and the branches swaying to and fro. Suddenly there was a big clash and a bang at the bottom of the road. Someone had been hurt. I rushed down to see them.

Danielle Jameson (11)
Huntington Secondary School

149

Control

Matthew Freeman was only fourteen years of age,
not the sort of boy to be sacrificed on a stone slab.
As the knife dropped he knew his life was limited.
He pleaded in his last moments. Just then the knife
glowed red. He knew he was in control.

Thomas Sutton (12)
Huntington Secondary School

150

The Weird Football

There was a boy that was rubbish at football. His dad
gave him a football. He said it was very old.
The next day he bought the football to the football
tryouts. They used the ball. He got picked because
the football was alive. He smiled.

Faysal Ahmad (12)
Huntington Secondary School

Run, Run

The alleyway was gloomy and dark. I pegged it down the alley, panting and breathing heavily. All to be seen was fish'n'chip wrappers from Kippers. I was scared, very scared. A figure pouncing towards me. still scared, I ran as fast as I could.
'Argh.'

Katie Bevan (12)
Huntington Secondary School

Viper's Worst Day

Viper was a blue Dodge Viper. All the water ran out in the city. Viper was depressed because he had a reputation for being a clean car. The problem was the mains had blown and water went everywhere. The mains were fixed and Viper was a clean car again.

Daniel Sewell (11)
Huntington Secondary School

A Show Rabbit's World

Stroke, brush, pat. Millions of eyes, staring. Bobtail the rabbit could hear others calling but she couldn't get to them. Some were happy, others distressed. A booming voice echoed. Being lifted out of her cage, being examined. Back in, back out. Something red flutters above her.

'First prize, pet show.'

Emma Alexander (12)
Huntington Secondary School

154

The Undiscovered Heroine

Silence, the only one there. Everyone else? Gone.
She stands alone in the dark abyss. No family, no
friends left but a country to protect. She grips the
gun, breathes and climbs over the top.
The undiscovered heroine.

Naomi Evans (12)
Huntington Secondary School

The Disguise

A large spaceship descended in front of Sophie. Out of it came two aliens. They writhed and seethed, constantly shape shifting.

'Come with us,' they said in unison.

Sophie turned and ran, screaming, into the night.

The aliens turned towards each other, 'I knew we should have been zebras!'

Bethany Cunnington (12)
Huntington Secondary School

Blood Trail

He walks into his house and sees blood across the
floor. He follows the trail of blood and sees his
brother on the floor. He goes over to him to see if he
is hurt. He turns around and hears a bang.
There was a gun in his brother's hand.

Graeme Quinlan (12)
Huntington Secondary School

The Fight That Was Lost

I'm nervous, heart thumping, fist aching. I've got my gloves at the ready, knees shaking. I get in the ring, mind-blowing. I get hit hard. Stomach growling. I fall to the floor, heartbroken.

Matthew Dearfove (12)
Huntington Secondary School

Who Killed Sally?

Creak! went the door. She tiptoed into the castle.
A sudden chill swept over the hallway. *Rip!*
A dilapidated tapestry fell to the floor. The trees
whistled in the gusty wind.
'Aaarrgh,' screamed Sally. She collapsed,
paralysed she lay.
She fell into a deep sleep, never to wake up again.

Jennifer Forshaw (12)
Huntington Secondary School

Christmas Time

It's Christmas time again. Jingle bells sounding, the bang of crackers and festive laughter. The ice and snow outside. After a long, cold day, I go to bed. Waiting for my presents in the morning. Maybe, just maybe, I will hear that ho, ho, ho, skip through the night.

Becca Dorking (13)
Huntington Secondary School

Snowflake

White and crispy, twirling to the ground, Christmas time is here. Snowmen are made by children. *Brrr!* It's cold outside.

Fluffy clouds all ready to burst from the sky, they fly, fly, fly! Inside, one special snowflake. It's a place called Whosville where the Grinch lives and tries to spoil Christmas!

Sammie Fraser (12)
Huntington Secondary School

The Fruit Disaster

Splosh! Splish! I was truly fruited. I threw an orange at Alex as she got a bat and hit it back. We broke windows and damaged stuff. I heard the neighbours talking to each other.
Ah! They called the police, so we made the great escape!

Jasmine Coffey (12)
Huntington Secondary School

Bye-Bye Bunny

He was a happy bunny, he was white with a pink tummy. He loved to be happy. But one day he woke up and felt very suicidal, so he told his family and they talked him out of it. But as he walked out of the door, *squash!* Bye-bye Bunny.

Eleanor Grace Kaloczi (12)

Huntington Secondary School

Sparta

300 went to war, looking for glory. Their rivals 1000,000 Persians were   also ready for glory. With the Spartan king, the formation was set like a spider, trapping them. With great military leadership they killed thousands.
A few days later they had gone, to celebrate they had won.

Adam MacLeffan (12)
Huntington Secondary School

Alien Teacher

'Good Morning!' *Ring, ring, ring,* goes the school bell, class is ready. There's a new teacher, *Zapp! Morph! Shock!* It's an alien. *Munch, gobble, scream,* the class is gone in one, eaten! *Boom, blast, zoom!* Off back into his home in space.

What's next?

Peter Ritchie (13)
Huntington Secondary School

Santa Is A Geordie

I lay asleep, there is no sound and then *crash!* I didn't move, frozen with fear, until I heard a voice. 'Ho, ho, ho and *howay* the lads.' It's then I realise Santa is a Geordie and is just not good enough at driving his sleigh.

Effie Thompson (13)
Huntington Secondary School

The Thing

It was an eerie night, with electric in the air. Jimmy was looking for his dog near the beck. He was alone. What was that? Extra strange sightings had been seen in this area …
Jimmy was scared. Red eyes glared at him - they came closer -
it was the thing. Attack!

Luke Charters-Reid (12)
Huntington Secondary School

Friend Or Foe

He crawled into the bunker to escape the wrath of the bombs that were being repeatedly dropped by the Nazis. He has an idea of what to do, but what exactly? Before he can think what to do someone crawled into the bunker.
Who? Friend or foe?

Mark Smith (12)
Huntington Secondary School

168

Heartbeat Of The Rabbit

A pair of neatly pointed ears stick out of the fog like a sore thumb. A man takes aim. The ears quiver. Run rabbit, run! A shot cuts through the air like a rock through a window. A thump is heard - the result of the rabbit's slow response. Heartbeat gone.

Lois Pacitto (13)
Huntington Secondary School

Three Little Pigs

One day, there were three little pigs who were moving out of their mother's house. So they went looking in the forest and found a tent. They set up camp and went to sleep. A butcher found them. Well let's just say they made nice sausages for my tea.

Jessica Russell (12)
Huntington Secondary School

Flash

Lights flashed and I went dizzy. Frozen to my seat.
I screamed, the shock took over and I was just sat
there, having flashbacks of what had happened.
I turned to look at my mum but she was slumped
over, motionless.

Faye Rich (13)
Huntington Secondary School

171

The Crash

Bang! There goes the 3rd engine, only one left now.
The plane gathered speed and plummeted forwards
towards the ground. I screamed as the ground grew
ever nearer. I was going to die!
Crash! Blackness. A tunnel, alight. It was over for me.
I'm dead, I just hang in limbo.

Katherine Wilson (12)
Huntington Secondary School

Saying Goodbye

It was time to say goodbye to my mum and sisters.
I hugged my mum and said bye. I realised I was
starting to fill up, my eyes were watery. I started to
feel a bit emotional. I felt happy one minute and the
next I was crying!

Kate Garnett (12)
Huntington Secondary School

Just Our Luck

Beth and Emma went ice skating together. When they got there the ice all turned to water. They thought well, let's go to Pizza Hut. It was closed. 'Why is it closed?' said Emma.
Just our luck. They walked down an alley, oh no, we're trapped in, 'Help!'

Annie Tysall (12)
Huntington Secondary School

World War I

The Blitz is blazing. Helicopters flying, the cannons
are blasting and people are falling down dead, like
they were never alive. The Germans are taking over
the city. A purely evil man with a moustache
in command.
This could be the end of the world as we know it.

Anthony Bundy (12)
Huntington Secondary School

Haunted Caravan

One night a caravan came alive, it screeched
and howled - moving around the field. Its wheel
screaming out loud. Coming to a halt near a village.
Barely making a sound. To the neighbours' fright,
there was no one there, except a caravan with a
rusty old scare.

Kelly Sockett (12)
Huntington Secondary School

The Duel

The cowboys withdrew their guns. They circled
each other like angry cats. They both clenched and
unclenched their fists.
The duel was about to begin.

Hoffie Davy (13)
Huntington Secondary School

Bang, I Got You

Let's go to shoot each other and beat the other
team. In we go to the dark, watch the boring video.
Then in we go, put on our armour and get out guns.
Then on the battlefield we take our place. Then off
we go and *bang!* I got you.

Jess Barnes (12)
Huntington Secondary School

178

Eid Was On Its Way

The swings were still, the trees bare. The ground glistened with a silvery morning frost but the sweet warm air told me that spring was on its way. 'Only one day to Eid,' shouted my sister. She raised both of her hands in the air and let out a cheer.

Sakina Variava (13)
Zakaria Muslim Girls High School

That Night

'Argh,' I screamed at the top of my lungs, as I woke
up and saw someone opening my door. Sweat
trickled down my face, like I had been running in the
Olympics. Its shadow came closer and closer, until it
was right near my bed.
Who could it be? Dad!

Mehwish Hussain (14)
Zakaria Muslim Girls High School

The Dreadful Night

It was a gloomy night. Alex was getting ready for bed.
She locked the doors and went up the stairs. She
checked that the kids were OK and was climbing into
bed, when suddenly, she felt a hand on her shoulder.
She turned and screamed as she fell into darkness.

Humayra Bismillah (15)
Zakaria Muslim Girls High School

The Big Fall

The fresh, clear air was pushing my face. My face was cold as ice, as I went up, moving side to side. The people were like tiny ants marching. My stomach was filled with butterflies. I was on the edge when suddenly, I fell over thousand feet on the Corkscrew.

Najifa Umarji (14)
Zakaria Muslim Girls High School

What Is She?

My heart was beating rapidly. I couldn't believe she was mine. At last I've got her, after many, many years of hard work.

'You're so beautiful,' I whispered lovingly to her. She was looking like a million dollars, sparkling like a precious diamond. She was the most gorgeous car ever.

Nafeesa Basser (14)
Zakaria Muslim Girls High School

Darling

I sat crying, as my kitten, that I'd adored so
much, died.
Next day my husband lay dying in my lap.
He said, 'I need to tell you something.'
I said, 'No, rest.'
He said, 'I killed your kitten.'
I said, 'Yes, I know, that's why I poisoned
you, darling!'

Naailah Iftikhar (15)
Zakaria Muslim Girls High School

184

An Unseen Ghost

It was a horrible, dark night, with rain and thunderstorms, owls howling in the trees. I was sleeping peacefully. Suddenly, I woke up with a start. What was that? I thought it sounded like a wolf. I couldn't believe what I saw, a ghost, in my garden!

Arfana Cheema (15)
Zakaria Muslim Girls High School

My Victim

I cornered her, my feeble victim. Sank my long, sharp teeth into her juicy neck. Drank her blood. It tasted like moist strawberries. When every last drop was finished, I let go of her white, bloodless body and went in search of my next powerless victim.

Anisah Mahmood (14)
Zakaria Muslim Girls High School

The Tunnel

She walked cautiously towards the inside of the uninviting, gloomy tunnel. Hearing only the sound of her own footsteps. A shadow emerged behind her, her footsteps got quicker and quicker. Then I heard a scream. I listened. There was nothing. No footsteps.

Mamoona Akhtar (14)
Zakaria Muslim Girls High School

70p For 870 (Real Life Event)

I went shopping. I bought a beautiful teapot and magazine costing 70p. I arrived home. I found £370 in the teapot. I was thrilled. I sat to do the crossword in the magazine. It was done, so I wrote my details and sent it.
A week later I received £500.

Mariam Akhtar (13)
Zakaria Muslim Girls High School

188

The Outsiders

'Argh!' I screamed in horror as two strange looking
aliens struck me with their extremely long,
black nails.
Suddenly, the immense fear within me diverted to an
optimistic hope. I fought courageously against them.
They were defeated in a measureless duration.
I couldn't believe myself.
I defeated them. I won.

Zeba Defair (14)
Zakaria Muslim Girls High School

My Nightmare

It was a cold, dark room. I could feel the shivers running down my spine. As I felt a hand touch my shoulder, I screamed for help as tears ran down my face. There was a spider in my room, with big feet. I turned and saw it was Spider-Man.

Nabeela Sirat (15)
Zakaria Muslim Girls High School

The Death

It was three weeks since Shayne had had his accident. He befriended Samuel, who spent his time describing the beautiful scenery outside the hospital, which was only a brick wall. Shayne recovered and went home.

Next day Shayne rang the hospital and learnt that Samuel had died and was blind.

Mubashsharah Kholvadia (16)
Zakaria Muslim Girls High School

YoungWriters

Information

We hope you have enjoyed reading this book - and that you will continue to enjoy it in the coming years.

If you like reading and writing, drop us a line or give us a call and we'll send you a free information pack. Alternatively visit our website at www.youngwriters.co.uk

Write to:
Young Writers Information,
Remus House,
Coltsfoot Drive,
Peterborough,
PE2 9JX
Tel: (01733) 890066
Email: youngwriters@forwardpress.co.uk